For all my piratical nephews and great-nephews,
old and young, with a great big grubalicious
"YO HO HO!" L.C.

For Dylan

First published in 2014 by Nosy Crow Ltd
The Crow's Nest, 10a Lant Street
London SE1 1QR
www.nosycrow.com

ISBN 978 0 85763 111 4 (HB)
ISBN 978 0 85763 112 1 (PB)

Nosy Crow and associated logos are trademarks and/or registered
trademarks of Nosy Crow Ltd.

Text copyright © Lucy Coats 2014
Illustrations copyright © Chris Mould 2014

The right of Lucy Coats to be identified as the author of this work
and of Chris Mould as the illustrator of this work has been asserted.

A CIP catalogue record for this book is available from the British Library.

Printed in China
Papers used by Nosy Crow are made from wood
grown in sustainable forests.

1 3 5 7 9 8 6 4 2 (HB)
1 3 5 7 9 8 6 4 2 (PB)

CAPTAIN BEASTLIE'S Pirate Party

nosy crow

Lucy Coats   Chris Mould

Captain Beastlie

was the grubbiest and smelliest pirate to sail the Seven Salty Seas.

But . . .

One grey and grimsome **Monday**, Captain Beastlie rolled out of bed. Five rotten cabbages rolled out, too.

"Only **5 days** left till m'birthday!" he roared, picking a bogey out of his nose and licking it.

"Take that, ye slimy scoundrel!"

5 days

On Tuesday,
Captain Beastlie
stomped up on deck.

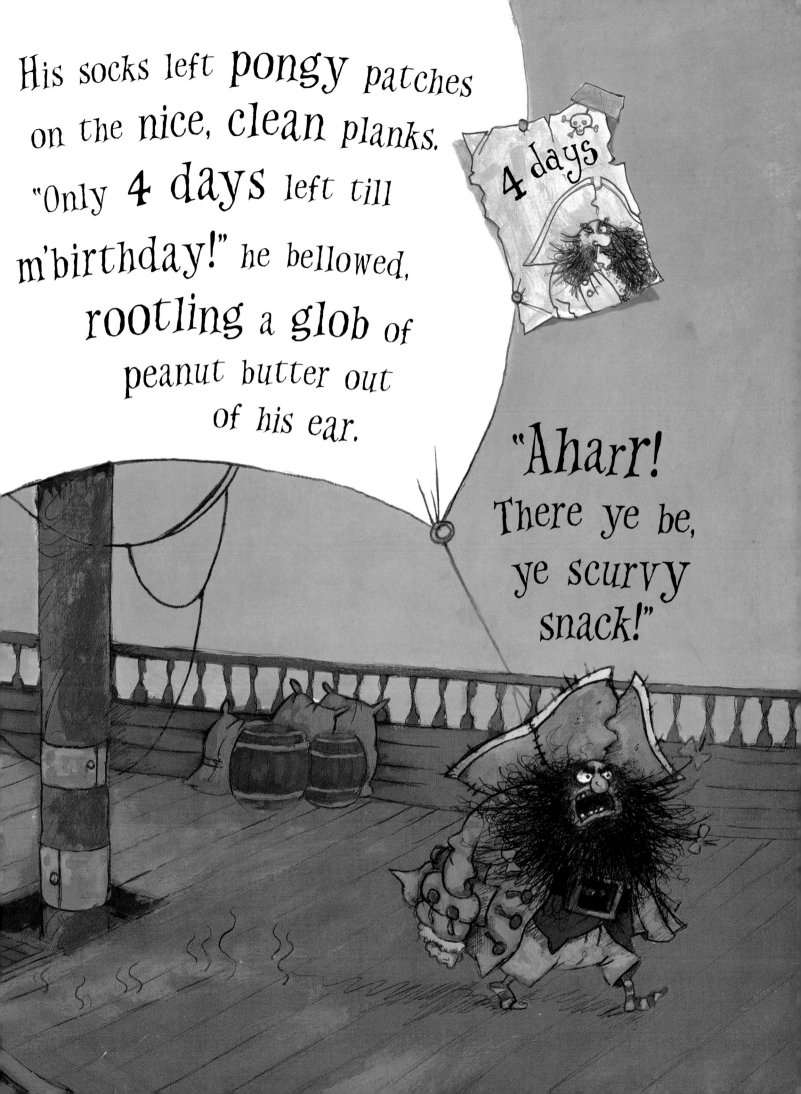

His socks left **pongy** patches on the nice, clean planks. "Only **4 days** left till m'birthday!" he bellowed, **rootling** a **glob** of peanut butter out of his ear.

4 days

"Aharr! There ye be, ye scurvy snack!"

On Wednesday, Captain Beastlie climbed the mast. His fingers left **filthy, green** fungus all over the **spotless** rigging. "Only **3 days** left till m'birthday," he hollered. Just then, his holey trousers let the breeze in around his bottom.

On Thursday, Captain Beastlie yelled for the ship's cook. "Only 2 days left till m'birthday!" he growled. "Where's the jam for my breakfast, ye lily-livered limpet?"

"All over yer jacket, Cap'n Beastlie, sir!" said the cook, saluting. Captain Beastlie rubbed his toast on his jacket, butter-side down. "Nummity-num!"

2 days

On Friday, Captain Beastlie kicked his mucky, messy clothes around the cabin. "Only 1 day left till m'birthday!" he chortled, sniffing a whiffy, rotten shirt. "Avast m'anchovies, that's luvverly!"

1 day

Late that night, there was a **rustling** and a **sneaking** all over the ship as his crew tiptoed about.

On Saturday, Captain Beastlie woke early. "Aharr! NO days to m'birthday!" he sang very loudly.

Then he stopped and looked round his cabin.

"Blustering bloodblisters! Where are all my luvverly, grubbly CLOTHES?" yelled Captain Beastlie, leaping out of bed to check his wardrobe.

Captain Beastlie stormed out of his cabin and out onto the deck . . .

"SCRUB-A-DUB-DUB! BIRTHDAY SURPRISE!"
shouted his crew, as they grabbed him and popped
him into a **big, bubbly** tub
and gave him a
big, bubbly
scrub.

BUCCANEER'S
BUBBLES

They combed out his **tangly** hair and beard . . .

. . . and wrapped him in a **clean** towel . . .

. . . then **Captain Beastlie** spotted a brightly-wrapped parcel.

Inside was . . .

... a brand new pirate suit
and hat.
"Happy Birthday to you!
Happy Birthday to you!

Happy Birthday, dear Cap'n—
Now you don't smell of poo!"
sang his crew.

Then they all sat down to a great, big skull cake birthday feast.

"Cheers, m'hearties!"

growled the

cleanest, shiniest

pirate to sail the

Seven Salty Seas . . .

. . . until he slurped

icky-sticky crumbs

all down his

brand new suit.

"Oops!"

said Captain Beastlie.